Long in the Tooth

Scully began to examine the wounds in Joe Goodensnake's lower chest and stomach area. "The shotgun wounds indicate point-blank range," she explained. "The pellets entered the body in a single mass. The assailant couldn't have been more than three feet away."

Mulder was barely listening. He knelt beside Goodensnake's head. Curious, he lifted the dead man's upper lip for a moment. Then he said, "We're going to need Goodensnake's dental records."

Scully and Tskany turned to him. "Why?" the sheriff asked.

This time Mulder pulled back both the upper and the lower lip. Tskany and Scully looked down at what Mulder had just seen: large, yellow fangs, each one an inch long.

THE Ⓧ FILES™

SHAPES

a novel by Ellen Steiber

based on the television series
The X-Files created by Chris Carter
based on the teleplay
written by Marilyn Osborn

HarperTrophy
A Division of HarperCollins*Publishers*

Thanks to Thomas Harlan, Mary Pappas, and Doug Lantz for invaluable computer aid, and to Munro Sickafoose for his generous sharing of Native American traditions.

This book is for Thomas, in hopes that next August won't be nearly so strange.

SHAPES

Chapter ONE

Two Medicine Ranch, Browning, Montana

Jim Parker had felt the storm building all day. The cattle had been restless that afternoon. The sun had set with a strange greenish tint. Now darkness had fallen, and the wind was up, howling like a man in pain. For the past hour, thunder had been rolling through the Montana skies. The rain hadn't hit yet. But it was coming.

Parker and his son, Lyle, stood inside by the door of the ranch house. They didn't speak. Instead they listened to the sounds of the storm. They were waiting for something. The thing that neither one of them had ever talked about. The thing that came to the ranch to kill.

Outside, lightning turned the black night sky to a silver white. As if the lightning had split open the clouds, rain began to fall in great windy sheets. And then the house went dark.

Parker wasn't bothered by the blackout. A fire blazed in the stone fireplace. It lit the room with an orange glow, reflecting in the glass eyes of the

1

hunting trophies that lined the walls. To Parker, the trophies were a comfort. The grizzly bear, the mountain lion, the timber wolf, the rattlesnake— they were all proof of the times he'd confronted danger and won. He intended to win again tonight.

And then Parker heard it. The same as he'd heard it the other times. A low, angry growl. Animal and yet not animal. There were times when Parker thought it sounded like an echo coming down from the mountains or rising up out of the earth itself.

The sound was closer now. Parker had hunted all his life. And though he didn't know exactly what was out there, he knew it was another hunter. Something that was hunting his cattle.

Tonight he wasn't taking any chances. Quickly he loaded twelve-gauge cartridges into the magazine of his Winchester 1300 Defender shotgun.

Parker's eyes met his son's. Lyle pumped the slide action of his shotgun. This time, they were ready for it.

Suddenly, from outside, the unearthly growl became a roar over the noise of the storm.

Lyle's head snapped toward the sound. Lightning flashed like a strobe light. In its harsh white glare, everything in the house seemed to be moving and still all at once. Lyle looked back at his father.

But Jim Parker was no longer aware of his son.

He was totally focused on whatever waited on the other side of the door.

Outside, storm winds swept across the ranch and rattled the leafless trees. A small group of cattle moved skittishly about the corral. They were afraid.

Guided by flashlight beams, Jim Parker and his son made their way toward the corral. The ground was already a pool of mud. Parker stayed dry in a long cowboy-style duster raincoat. But Lyle, who wore jeans and a down vest, was soaked through. He shivered a little, not sure if it was from the cold or from fear of meeting whatever it was they'd come out there to meet.

Parker signaled to Lyle that he'd take the left side of the barn. Lyle nodded, going to the right.

Then he tensed as he heard it.

Something in the darkness was growling.

The sound seemed to be coming from the open barn. Slowly Lyle approached the wide doorway. His heart was hammering. He hoped the creature hadn't gone after the horses.

Gripping the shotgun in one hand and a flashlight in the other, he stepped inside the barn. He felt a little calmer as he was greeted by the familiar sweet smell of hay and the sounds of the horses. He checked the stalls. The horses were nervous but unharmed. Storms always made them skittish.

Carefully Lyle searched the rest of the barn. He felt himself taking deep breaths, trying to slow his racing heart.

In the darkness, a creature crept up behind him. A creature Lyle never saw. It walked on two legs. Its limbs seemed human in shape. But it moved with an animal's power. And in the lightning, its claws shone like ivory razors.

The barn was clear, Lyle decided. He walked back outside and stopped as he spotted something on the ground. A dark heap. He started toward it, unaware that animal eyes were tracking him, their irises bloodred.

Lyle shone his flashlight on the heap. His heart sank. They were too late. It was another cow. Dead, its hide ripped to shreds. He stood over it, sad and frightened. What kind of animal could mutilate a cow this way? And how were they ever going to stop it?

He heard the sound again. This time right behind him.

Lyle swung the flashlight and caught the eyes of the beast in its light. Inhuman red eyes.

He didn't have time to raise his weapon before the creature attacked, slamming him down. Lyle hit the ground hard, then felt his body lifted into the air. Tossed like a rag doll by something unseen in the darkness.

The last thing Lyle Parker remembered was the sound of his own screams mixing with the roar of the creature—as he crashed through the corral fence.

Jim Parker heard a struggle in the barn area and he raced toward it, hoping he'd get to his cattle before the predator did.

His eyes widened with terror when he saw a huge two-legged creature, its back covered with a thick pelt. It was attacking his son.

Parker didn't hesitate. He raised his gun and fired. The animal twisted from the impact, then fell to the ground.

Parker knelt by Lyle's side. The boy was bloodied and shaking, but he was alive.

Then Lyle did something he hadn't done since he was ten years old. He put his arms around his father and clung on as if he'd never let go.

Parker held him for a moment, but his mind was on the creature. It was lying perfectly still, not ten feet across the corral. But he didn't trust it to be dead. Just to be sure, Parker turned and pumped the shotgun once more into its body.

Lightning flashed again. To his horror, Parker saw just what it was he'd killed. Not an animal, but a man. A young Native American man, bare-chested, with long, black hair. He looked to be about twenty-five years old. About the same age as Lyle.

Parker felt himself start to tremble with shock. He'd been sure he was shooting at an animal. But he'd just killed a man.

Chapter TWO

Two days later FBI agents Fox Mulder and Dana Scully left the agency headquarters in Washington, D.C., and flew to northwest Montana. They were investigating the death of a young Trego Indian man named Joe Goodensnake. Two Medicine Ranch was their first stop.

Scully was at the wheel of the rental car as they drove down the long dirt road that crossed the range and led to the ranch house. "Nice spread Parker has here," she observed.

"Five thousand acres," Mulder said. "He's got one of the most profitable ranches in this part of the country."

"And a home that looks like a hunting lodge," Scully said as the sprawling two-story log house came into view.

Jim Parker met them at the door and ushered them into the living room. Mulder immediately took in the surroundings: the stone fireplace, the high cathedral ceiling, the picture window that looked out on the vast range. Unlike many ranchers, the Parkers lived well.

Jim Parker was in his fifties, with gray collar-length hair, a handlebar mustache, and dark, piercing eyes. He had the rugged, weathered look of a man who had spent his life working outdoors—and the brusque manner of a man who was used to being in control.

Parker introduced them to his son, Lyle, and his lawyer, David Gates. Lyle was a good-looking young man who appeared to be in his early twenties. Mulder studied him with interest. Lyle had a softer quality than his father. Mulder suspected that where Jim Parker might make a snap decision, Lyle would think things through.

They sat down in the living room. A fire burned in the fireplace; the mantel held a clock and some photographs. But there was nothing warm or inviting about the room. It was actually a little . . . disturbing. Because what stood out more than the roaring fire was the animals.

Clearly, Mulder thought, *Parker was not only a rancher but a hunter.* The room was filled with mounted hunting trophies. A grizzly bear stood upright in one corner of the room, frozen in mid-attack. A great horned owl, its wings spread, perched near the ceiling. A badger stood on a coffee table, a kit fox on top of a bookcase. A wolf, fangs bared, lunged from a corner. The people in the room were surrounded by dead animals.

Mulder sat next to Gates, the lawyer. Scully sat across from them, on the other side of a coffee table. Lyle stood behind his father, looking concerned. Parker paced the room as he gave the agents his side of the story. "I am *not* a killer," he began.

Mulder's eyes went to the mounted animals. *That all depends on what kind of killer*, he thought.

"And I never meant to hurt no one," Parker went on. "I was just getting fed up with my cattle bein' butchered a hundred miles from the slaughterhouse. That's the fourth one in the last month alone!" he said angrily.

"And who, or what, did you suspect was responsible?" Mulder asked calmly.

"Look, mister," Parker said heatedly. "That cow looked like a piece of paper gone through a shredder. I don't know of no animal that could've done that."

"Then are you saying you believe a person, or persons, was responsible for this?" Mulder asked.

Gates, a balding middle-aged man wearing a jacket and a bolo tie, spoke up. "I want to remind you that Mr. Parker is free on bail pending trial. He's agreed to speak to you. But only about this incident and not about any other pending case."

"So we can't talk about Mr. Parker's federal court case against the Trego Indian Reservation?" Scully asked.

Mulder saw the lawyer's face redden at Scully's question. Scully was a pretty young woman with reddish blond hair and deep blue eyes. Most people never guessed how tough she was—until they had to deal with her.

"That's exactly what it means," Gates snapped.

"Now, wait just a second," Jim Parker broke in.

"Jim, don't say a word," Gates warned.

"No, this ain't the time for that lawyer stuff," Parker said sharply. "I want to get this out in the open."

Parker's honesty was admirable, Mulder thought. Yet the man was unlikable. It wasn't only that he was impatient and angry. Something in his manner made it clear that he was used to getting his own way. And would bully everyone in sight until he did.

Parker glared at the two agents. "You people think I went out and killed me an Indian just because we're having an argument over where my land ends and their land begins?"

"We want to settle that peacefully," Lyle insisted in a quiet tone. "In court."

"Well, Joseph Goodensnake is dead with wounds from *your* shotgun," Scully reminded Jim Parker. "Which indicates otherwise."

The rancher calmed down a little. "All I'm saying

is, it was no kind of animal that *I know of*," he explained. "And that night, it sure didn't seem human either. Take a look at my boy's scars."

Lyle lifted his shirt, looking a little embarrassed. A network of grotesque stitches and gashes covered his shoulder and chest.

Mulder was not surprised.

"It was dark," Jim Parker went on. "And we heard a growl. We went out to protect the cattle." He sat down, and his voice became a little less defensive. For the first time he sounded unsure. "I could've sworn I saw red eyes and fangs."

Mulder saw a skeptical expression in Scully's eyes. Scully didn't put a lot of stock in monster stories.

"I thought my boy Lyle was . . ." Parker couldn't finish the sentence. He shook his head as if he still couldn't believe what he'd seen. "Look, nobody, *nobody* was more shocked and upset than I was to find out it was that young Indian boy." The rancher's voice became stronger, his tone accusing. "But if he was the one killing our cattle, I'm very, very sorry we had to find out in such a way, but . . . As far as I'm concerned, that's the end of it."

Mulder nodded neutrally. Parker's attitude reminded him of every old Western he'd ever seen. If

Joe Goodensnake was killing cattle, then Parker had a right to protect his property.

Scully sent Mulder a questioning look, as if to say, "Do you believe him?"

Mulder gave her a quick nod. He was certain Parker was telling the truth—as he knew it. Mulder was also certain there was a good deal more to the story.

Chapter THREE

Scully had read the police report on Joe
Goodensnake's death. She had listened to every
word Jim Parker had said. And she still didn't
understand why she and Mulder were investigating
this case. To her, this seemed like a straightforward
homicide. There was no mystery. Parker even
admitted he'd killed Goodensnake. It was the sort of
case Mulder was usually glad to let other agents
handle.

Mulder had a special interest in the kinds of
cases that no other agent in the bureau would
touch. They were called the X-Files, and they dealt
with the weird, the paranormal, and the supernatural.

Scully was trained as a medical doctor and a
physicist. She was a scientist who believed in the
laws of cause and effect, in rational explanations.
But there was nothing rational about the X-files.
Working with Mulder, she'd investigated aliens,
mutants, and psychic visions that somehow became
real. Things she could barely believe, even when
she'd seen the evidence with her own eyes.

Lots of people in the bureau thought Mulder was nuts. They even called him Spooky behind his back. But they didn't get rid of him. Mulder was too good an agent. He had a photographic memory. He was brilliant when it came to analyzing cases, Scully thought, even if he was a little too eager to believe in the supernatural. But there was nothing supernatural about this case. So what were they doing here in Browning, Montana?

Now Mulder stood up. "Can we see the corral?" he asked Parker.

"I'll take you out there," Lyle offered.

He put on a jacket, grabbed his hat, and led the two agents outside through a sliding glass door that opened onto the porch.

Scully pulled up the collar of her raincoat. A drizzle was falling, and the scent of pine trees filled the air. Back in D.C., the temperature had been in the seventies. Here, in the shadow of the Rocky Mountains, it was cold and damp. It felt more like winter than fall.

She was glad, though, that they were getting a chance to talk to Lyle alone. Of the two Parkers, he was the one who seemed genuinely upset about the death of Joe Goodensnake.

The boy led them a short distance from the house and then stopped. "Agent Mulder. Agent Scully," he said hesitantly. "I suppose if I were hearin' our side of the story, it might not hold up too well. There's parts of it I don't understand myself. Things my father could never try to explain to a stranger."

"What kinds of things?" Mulder asked.

Lyle hesitated. When he finally spoke, he did so rapidly, as if his thoughts had been bottled up for a long time and were finally spilling out.

"For the last few months," he said, "whenever we'd go outside at night and check on the cattle . . . I never saw anything out of the ordinary. Not a mountain lion. Not a coyote. Not even any Tregos."

He sighed, his breath clouding up in the cold air. "But I could feel it," he said. "Something not human. Out there." He nodded toward the mountains. "Watching me. The air was more still. The night animals more quiet. It was like Nature herself was terrified."

Lyle shook his head, as if ashamed to admit these things. "It gave me the creeps."

"The creeps?" Scully asked doubtfully.

"Yeah. The creeps," Lyle said. "Don't you ever get the creeps?"

Scully shrugged. "The creeps" was not a concept she thought about very often. Irrational fear, which was probably what Lyle was talking about, was simply not something Scully had time for.

Mulder shot her an accusing look, as if to say, "You can give him a better answer than that."

Let Mulder talk about the creeps if he wants to, Scully thought. She was more interested in investigating at the scene of the crime. Briskly she set off for the corral.

A light rain continued to fall as Scully finished her examination of the barn. For the last time, she checked the police report. Satisfied that the police hadn't missed anything, she opened her umbrella and crossed the corral. She stopped a moment to look at a spot where the fence was down. Lyle had told her it had broken when his attacker had thrown him against it.

Mulder stood on the other side of the muddy corral. He was looking off into the mountains as if they held some message for him.

Scully glanced at the report again and stood in front of the broken fence.

"The victim was shot here," she called to Mulder. "About three meters from where Jim Parker fired." She shook her head as she thought of the rancher's version of the shooting. "There's no way he could have mistaken a person for an animal at that close range. This is open and shut, Mulder."

Mulder stared at the ground, unmoving.

"You know, I'm surprised you volunteered for this assignment," Scully went on. "Any bureau agent could have investigated this homicide. Why *are* you interested?"

Mulder stared at a muddy area marked up with tracks. Cattle hoofprints mixed with the prints from a man's boots. And then Mulder found what he was looking for.

He knelt to get a better look. Carefully he traced the human prints. They went from boot prints to bare footprints. And then they changed again—into the tracks of a large, clawed animal. From one step to the next. Human to beast.

He snapped a photograph of the prints. He'd been expecting evidence like this. Then he spotted something he hadn't expected. Something he hadn't even imagined.

Scully wrapped up her investigation of the crime scene and strode toward Mulder. "The Tregos and the Parkers are fighting over land," she reminded him. "Goodensnake had a motive to attack Parker's cattle. And Parker had a motive to kill Goodensnake. There seems to be nothing unexplainable about this case."

"Nope," Mulder agreed in a dry tone. "Not a thing."

Scully's eyebrows rose as Mulder held up his surprising discovery with a pair of tweezers. It was a piece of translucent skin—in the shape of a three-fingered hand.

Chapter FOUR

Scully gazed out at the landscape as Mulder drove their rental car toward the Trego Indian Reservation. The road stretched ahead of them, flat and endless. Dried brown grasses lined it. There were no buildings, no gas stations, no telephone poles. Nothing except the black strip of tarmac to hint that humans had ever touched this land. Ahead of them the Rockies soared, dark and foreboding.

Everything was so spread out in the West, Scully thought. Parker's ranch bordered the reservation, but to reach the town in the center of the reservation, she and Mulder had been driving well over an hour.

Once again, Scully examined the plastic evidence bag that held the bizarre piece of skin.

"Mulder, this is so odd," she said. "It's almost like a snake skin that's been shed."

Mulder just nodded.

Scully set the evidence bag on the dashboard. "I suspect that the Parkers knowingly killed Joe Goodensnake," she said. "But they hardly seem the type to skin their victims."

"Besides, police and coroner's reports make no mention of such an act," Mulder agreed.

"Well, we're going to have to take a look at the body ourselves," Scully said. As both a doctor and an FBI agent, Scully often performed autopsies.

"The body's been transferred to the reservation authorities," Mulder said. He dug into his jacket pocket, fished out a slip of paper, and laid it against the center of the steering wheel. "We're supposed to get in touch with a Sheriff Charlie Tskany. . . ."

Mulder's voice trailed off as a harsh cawing drew his attention. He looked up at the sky, where an eagle soared across the landscape. Mulder pulled over to the side of the road.

"What are you doing?" Scully asked.

"Taking a minute to watch the eagle," Mulder said. "You don't see too many of those in D.C."

He got out of the car and looked around. Clouds of mist shrouded the mountain peaks. Mulder had a distinct sense of this land's being very old. Of its having been a silent witness to history long before white people came to America. He couldn't help feeling as though the mist were cloaking ancient mysteries and secrets.

A wind blew through the evergreens up on the mountains. Storm clouds gathered before the sun. The eagle cawed again, and a flock of crows took flight.

Mulder knew that Scully would say those things didn't add up to anything. But he felt a presence. And it spooked him.

"Mulder!" Scully said loudly.

Mulder snapped out of it and looked at her, a bit dazed.

"You all right?" Scully asked.

"The devil just touched my spine," Mulder said quietly.

"What?"

"My mother used to say, if you felt a shiver, 'The devil just touched your spine,' " Mulder explained.

Scully shrugged, not really following.

"You know, Scully," Mulder said, "you never answered Lyle Parker's question. I'm interested. Don't you ever get the creeps?"

Scully considered the question a bit impatiently. "When I'm on the subway in D.C. at three in the morning," she admitted.

"No, that's clear and present danger," Mulder said. "The creeps is about being aware of a presence you can't see or hear."

Now Scully's patience was gone. "Mulder, look around," she said. "There are trees. Mountains. Animals. It's beautiful . . . meditative. But the creeps come from your psyche, probably suggested by Lyle Parker's attempt at an alibi."

Mulder gave her a look of disbelief. "Have you ever been to Niagara Falls?" he demanded.

"When I was a girl," Scully said.

"Do you know the geologic explanation of their origin?"

Scully thought back to her classes in earth science. "I believe the retreat of melting glaciers some ten thousand years ago enabled water from Lake Erie to flow into Ontario, which, I assume, has a lower elevation."

Mulder nodded. He'd expected an explanation like that. Dana Scully was a scientist through and through. Still, he couldn't resist challenging her.

"But when you're standing at the base of Niagara Falls," he said, "don't you just sense there's more to it? Can't you feel the presence of something else at work?"

"Of course," Scully said. "Gravity."

Irked, Mulder turned away. He froze as he saw a red-tailed hawk perched on the hood of the car. Its wings were fully extended—an ominous warning. The bird gazed at him and then suddenly flew off, leaving the two agents alone on the road.

"The Plains Indians believe hawks are the spirits of inner strength needed to fight evil," Mulder said.

Scully's eyes followed the flying hawk. "Mulder," she said, "it's just a hawk."

Mulder shot her a look, then got into the car. Scully followed, shaking her head.

A short time later, after miles of wilderness, the two agents drove into the small town in the middle of the Trego Reservation. The wide dirt road had turned to mud in the rain. One side was lined with trailers and small frame houses. The other side was the business center: a convenience store, coin laundry, post office, pool hall. At the very end of the strip was a gas station.

Mulder noted a number of pickup trucks, a couple of motorcycles, and one satellite antenna dish. Dogs ran loose everywhere, some following the people as they went about their business, some running in packs. But there were few luxuries in sight. Like many Native Americans who lived on reservations, the Trego people did not have a lot of money.

"Where do we start?" Scully asked as Mulder parked the car.

"Let's try the pool hall," he suggested.

The inside of the pool hall was dark. Blinds covered the windows. A neon sign flickered over the counter. In the dimness Mulder could see three large rooms. Crowded tables and chairs filled most of the floor space. In a side room a ratty pool table covered in worn green felt stood beneath a single lightbulb. A young woman wearing jeans, a flannel shirt, and a tan vest was shooting pool. There was no jukebox. A Johnny Cash song played on a boom box behind the counter. The place smelled of smoke and coffee and damp wool.

Though it was the middle of the day, most of the tables were filled. Except for the two agents, everyone in the pool hall was Native American. As Mulder and Scully started toward the bar, a man bumped into Mulder—deliberately. Mulder let it go.

The pool hall fell silent as the two agents walked through. Their white skin and business suits marked them immediately as outsiders. They were not welcome here. And they both knew it.

Mulder wasn't bothered by feeling like an outsider. He'd felt that way most of his life, even within the FBI. But he was bothered by the reason behind the Tregos' hostility. White people had a long, tragic history of treating Indian people terribly. They'd driven them from their homes, taken their land, and in some cases massacred them. Mulder didn't blame the people here for not trusting him. He just wished he could undo some of the damage.

A waiter stood behind the counter, pouring coffee for a customer.

Mulder cleared his throat. "'Scuse me," he said. "We're not from around here. We're looking for Sheriff Tskany?"

The waiter didn't reply. He finished pouring the

coffee, then walked away. The only response was Johnny Cash's voice singing about love and loss.

"Does anyone know Charlie Tskany?" Mulder tried again. He spoke loudly enough so that everyone in the place could hear him.

No one answered. Mulder scanned the crowd patiently. It was a small community. Most of the people in the pool hall probably knew the sheriff. It was just a matter of finding one person who would answer his questions.

In the corner, a group of young men in their twenties were acting as if he and Scully didn't exist. They all wore denim jackets and heavy-metal T-shirts.

The young woman who was playing pool straightened up. She had long, wavy brown hair and a strong, determined face. She was glaring daggers at the agents. *Nope,* Mulder thought. *Not a great candidate for giving answers.*

He checked back with Scully. She gestured with a nod that she thought they ought to go.

But Mulder waited a moment longer.

And then an eerie voice broke the silence and spoke three words: "Go home, FBI."

Chapter FIVE

Mulder turned in the direction of the voice. Off to his left, two older men sat at a table in a darkened corner. Mulder moved toward them.

The man who had spoken had long, silver-gray hair, broad cheekbones, and copper-colored skin. He wore a plaid wool jacket, and beneath it a denim shirt. A beaded choker circled his neck. Mulder detected something in his eyes that he'd encountered maybe once or twice in his life. A particular kind of calm and clarity. There was very little, Mulder sensed, that could frighten this man. He'd seen too much.

And his words intrigued Mulder. "How'd you know I'm FBI?" Mulder asked.

"I could smell you a mile away," the man answered.

"Ah. They tell me that even though my deodorant's made for a woman, it's strong enough for a man," Mulder joked.

The Trego man didn't seem to think the joke was funny. "I was at Wounded Knee in 1973," he said, as if that explained everything.

In fact, it told Mulder a good deal about him. Mulder knew about the confrontation—and the one that had come before it.

In 1973, Native Americans seized the village of Wounded Knee and challenged the U.S. government to repeat a massacre that had taken place there nearly a hundred years before. They were promptly surrounded by heavily armed agents of the federal government. After seventy-two days, the Indians surrendered. But they'd brought nation-wide attention to their tragedies of the past—and the present.

"And what I learned fighting the FBI," the Trego man continued, "is you don't believe in us. And we don't believe in you."

"I want to believe," Mulder said, echoing the words of the poster that hung in his office. For Mulder it was the truth. He wanted to believe in things that were often denied and ridiculed. Those things included the beliefs of people—like the Native Americans—who didn't always agree with the government.

The old man studied Mulder, his eyes suspicious. "Why are you here? What are you looking for?"

"I think you already know what we're looking for," Mulder answered. Although he'd never seen the Trego man before, he felt a connection with him, as if they understood each other.

"You tell me what I know," the man challenged.

Scully stepped forward. Mulder and the old man were talking in strange riddles. She needed direct answers. "We're looking for any individuals who might be able to provide information on the homicide of Joe Gooden—"

"We're looking for whatever can create a human track in one step and an animal track in the next," Mulder said, cutting her off.

"Parker," the Trego man said at once. "*He* found what you're looking for. He *killed* what you're looking for, FBI."

Suddenly the young woman in the tan vest slammed her pool cue down against the table. The two agents whirled around.

"What Parker and his kid killed was *my brother*," she said furiously. "And you're all too afraid of some stupid Indian legend to do anything. I hate it!"

"Gwen!" the old man said.

The woman ignored him. She grabbed her jacket and headed for the door. But she stopped for a moment in front of Mulder and Scully.

"And I hate suits who are always here when *they* want something from *us*. But when we need help, they're nowhere to be found."

As Scully watched her leave, she noticed a Native American man wearing a jacket with a sheriff's badge and patch on the shoulder. He was tall, with fine, even features and graying hair combed straight back. He'd been standing in the shadows, silently watching them.

"Sheriff Tskany?" Scully guessed.

He looked at her without expression.

Scully stepped forward, relieved to have found another law officer. "I'm Agent Scully. This is Agent Mulder."

The sheriff nodded. He seemed no more welcoming than anyone else in the village.

"Goodensnake's body is in my office," he said in clipped tones. He turned and left the pool hall without giving them a chance to respond.

Scully and Mulder exchanged a look. They were both a little surprised by the sheriff's coolness. There was nothing to do, though, except follow him to the body of Joe Goodensnake.

Chapter SIX

Scully and Mulder walked behind Sheriff Tskany to a weathered, wooden building. The lettering on the glass door read TRIBAL POLICE OFFICE.

Two Trego men stood on the stairs, flanking the door. They were dressed in jeans, shirts, jackets, and boots. They both had long, black hair, which they worc braided. A feather was tied to the end of each braid. But it was their faces that made Mulder stare. From a distance, he'd thought they were wearing white masks. Up close, he saw that they'd painted their faces with white ashes. The effect was eerie. Ghostly.

Charlie Tskany started up the stairs to his office. Mulder and Scully were right behind him. The two ghostly men moved together, blocking their way.

"Bill, Tom, let them through," the sheriff said in a quiet voice. "C'mon, boys, let 'em through."

The two men waited a moment, then moved aside.

The reservation police office was nothing like the big-city station houses Mulder and Scully were used to. There weren't dozens of overworked cops rushing around. There were no phones ringing, people shouting complaints, or suspects waiting to be booked. There was no chaos and no noise.

It was one simple room. A chair. A filing cabinet. A single empty jail cell in the back corner. In the center, a desk with a computer and a phone on it.

Tskany went to the desk and looked through a pile of mail.

Mulder gestured toward the men at the door. "Who are they?" he asked.

"Guardians of the dead," Tskany answered. "They escort the deceased spirit to the next world." He stepped behind his desk. "I only let them as far as the front door," he said. "Anybody that knows me, knows I keep the ancient beliefs out there, the police work in here."

Something was bothering Mulder. "The woman in the pool hall said that people were afraid of some Indian legend. What do they believe happened in the Parker case?"

The sheriff studied the two Washington agents.

"Look," he said. "I'm not a park ranger here to answer all your questions about Indians."

Mulder tried to explain that that was not what he'd meant. But Tskany cut him off. "Whenever I need federal help, I never get it. Since this case falls under the jurisdiction of the FBI, you're entitled to examine the body. So let's get it over with."

Mulder and Scully exchanged a glance. Jurisdiction was a touchy subject. The Indian reservations were independent, with their own tribal governments, laws, police, and constitutions. But when a felony was committed, the federal government had the right to step in.

Mulder knew that what Tskany was saying was true. Too often, the government showed no interest in problems on the reservations. And now he and Scully weren't here because the Tregos had asked for help. They were here because Mulder had taken an interest in the case. To the Tregos, it felt like interference.

Tskany opened a door at the other end of the room. Mulder and Scully followed him through it.

A body, covered by a sheet, lay on a table. The handwriting on the toe tag read JOE GOODENSNAKE.

"Was the woman in the pool hall his sister?" Mulder asked.

"Gwen?" Tskany asked. "Yeah, she and Joe are primarily responsible for fueling the boundary dispute with Parker. They felt he'd been grazing his cattle farther and farther onto the reservation. Parker probably told you it was his idea to settle it in court. But Joe and Gwen filed the suit."

31

Mulder pulled back the sheet that covered the body. He saw a good-looking young man with a high forehead and long, black hair.

"Mulder," Scully said, "take a look at that scar tissue. It looks like *he's* been attacked by an animal as well."

Three long, raised lines of scar tissue curved around Joe Goodensnake's shoulder and ran down his chest. Mulder nodded, as if this were another piece of the puzzle fitting neatly into place.

Tskany, though, looked surprised. "Could Joe have been attacked also? Maybe the Parkers *did* see an animal."

"No," Scully said. "These wounds have been healing for quite some time. If Goodensnake was attacked, it happened a long time ago."

She began to examine the wounds in the lower chest and stomach area. "The shotgun wounds indicate point-blank range," she explained. "The pellets entered the body in a single mass. The assailant couldn't have been more than three feet away."

Mulder was barely listening. He knelt beside Goodensnake's head. Curious, he lifted the dead man's upper lip for a moment. Then he said, "We're going to need Goodensnake's dental records."

Scully and Tskany turned to him. "Why?" the sheriff asked.

This time Mulder pulled back both the upper and the lower lip. Tskany and Scully looked down at what Mulder had just seen: large, yellow fangs, each one an inch long.

Chapter SEVEN

A short time later, Mulder stood in Tskany's office, examining Joe Goodensnake's dental X rays. He held them up in front of a desk lamp. Goodensnake's body lay on a gurney a few feet behind them.

Mulder pointed to the X ray. "See, these are the canine cuspids. They're normal."

Scully tried to make sense of that, considering the large catlike fangs they'd just seen in Goodensnake's mouth. "Well, could the records have been switched or mislabeled?" she asked.

Mulder shook his head. "No. You see, the second incisor here is chipped, just like the one in his mouth. These X rays match Joe Goodensnake's."

Scully paused, searching for a medical explanation. "Well, there are cases of calcium phosphate salts developing abnormally with age . . ."

Mulder nodded, neither agreeing nor disagreeing.

Charlie Tskany spoke up. "That could account for what Jim Parker claims to have seen. He was out that night, expecting to see a mountain lion killing his cattle. He gets rattled, and a flashlight beam catches Joe here—" He pointed to Goodensnake's mouth.

"So Parker saw what he wanted to see," Scully said, continuing Tskany's thought. "An animal."

Mulder wasn't sold on this theory. "Lyle Parker was attacked by something," he reminded them. "He has scars just like Joe's."

Mulder turned to the sheriff. "Do you have a facility where we can perform an autopsy?"

"Why?" Tskany asked.

"Well, if Joe's teeth are abnormal, an autopsy may reveal abnormalities in the interior of his anatomy as well," Mulder answered. "I'd be interested to see what his heart and other organs look like."

"I can't allow that," Tskany said, returning to his desk. Mulder got the distinct idea that for Tskany, the investigation was over.

Scully trailed after the sheriff, unwilling to give up. "I'm fully qualified," she assured him.

"No," Tskany said firmly. "I can't let you do an autopsy. The funeral's tonight."

"It's a cremation," Mulder said. "After that, we'll have nothing."

Tskany gave a tired sigh. "The Tregos believe the recent dead are unsettled by their new condition as spirits," he explained. "Any desecration of the body angers the spirit and keeps it haunting this world."

Scully couldn't believe that Tskany would let religious beliefs get in the way of a criminal investigation. Especially beliefs in ghosts!

"But you're a law enforcement officer," she argued. "You can't destroy evidence."

"Don't tell me what I can't do," the sheriff said angrily. "Native Americans believe that there are laws greater and more just than those of the U.S. government."

He glared at the two agents, allowing his point to settle in. "If they want Joe at rest, rather than cut up as a piece of evidence, that's the way it's gonna be," he went on. "And if you want to make an issue out of it with your 'higher authority,' go right ahead."

Scully looked at Mulder. She knew that as the federal agent in charge of this investigation, he could push for the autopsy. She also knew that he wouldn't. Mulder, too, believed there were laws that mattered more than those of the government. Mulder had his own unwritten laws, which he followed no matter what. And one of them was being open to and respectful of the beliefs of others.

"Charlie," Mulder said curiously. "Do you believe that the spirit of Joe Goodensnake is in that room?"

The sheriff eyed them warily. Scully guessed that he really did believe it, but would never admit it to federal agents.

Finally Tskany answered. "All I know is that tomorrow, day after, you're gonna leave. But I have to stay here. I've got to answer to these people. Now, you can continue your investigation, but you'll have to do it without Joe Goodensnake's body."

Chapter EIGHT

Scully and Mulder reached the burial ground well before dark. The ceremony was being held in a clearing, high on a hilltop above the village. The place was both beautiful and desolate. There was nothing else in sight except pine forest. And a clear view of the darkening clouds.

The preparations for the ceremony had already begun. Joe Goodensnake lay atop a rectangular burial platform built of logs and branches. His body was wrapped in a white shroud. The two white-faced guardians of the dead stood in front of the pyre. A medicine man, wearing a wolf's skin and waving an eagle feather, circled the body.

Mulder had been lucky enough to have observed several other Native American ceremonies. He knew that eagles were considered birds of great power. Because no other creature flew so high, many Indians believed that the eagle carried prayers and messages to the spirits who lived beyond the clouds. As Mulder watched the medicine man circle the pyre with the feather, he knew that powerful prayers were being sent up to help Joe Goodensnake's spirit on its journey.

Mulder and Scully sat in their rental car, watching. One by one the mourners began to arrive. Gwen Goodensnake, dressed in black jeans and a black jacket, stood near her brother's body.

"Mulder," Scully said in a troubled voice. "Ever since we've been here, you've acted as if you *expected* to find every piece of evidence we've come across. What aren't you telling me? Why are we here?"

Mulder considered her question for a moment. Then he reached to the backseat, where his briefcase lay. He took out a dog-eared, yellowed file with old typewriter script on the cover.

"A true piece of history, Scully," he said. "The very first X-file. Initiated by J. Edgar Hoover himself in 1946." He handed her the folder and began to summarize the case. "During World War Two, a series of murders occurred in and around the Northwest. Seven here in Browning alone."

Scully examined the wrinkled pages of the file.

"Each victim was basically ripped to shreds and eaten, as if by a wild animal," Mulder went on. "However, many of the victims were found in their homes, as if they had allowed the killer to enter."

Scully listened without comment.

"In 1946, police cornered what they believed to be such an animal in a cabin in Glacier National Park. They shot it. But when they went in to retrieve the carcass, they found only the body of Richard Watkins."

"Sounds like the Parker scenario," Scully said. "The murders stopped that year," Mulder said. "Because the cases were unsolved and considered so bizarre, Hoover locked them away, hoping that in time, people around here would forget about them."

Scully skimmed through the pages of the file. "This indicates that the same type of murders started again in 1954," she said.

"And '59, '64, '78, and now again in '94. But . . ." Mulder reached back and rooted through his briefcase.

"Here it comes," Scully said. She'd been working with Mulder long enough to recognize his tone of voice. Any second now, he would go into one of his weird theories: Aliens on the reservation. Psychic mountain lions. Or . . .

Mulder produced another file, a more recent one. "These man-animal–related murders predate the oldest X-file by one hundred and fifty years," he told her.

Scully flipped through the papers and photos that Mulder had gathered. He'd photocopied pages from old journals. The first one was dated 1805 in a flowing script.

"Members of the Lewis and Clark expedition

wrote of Indian men who could change their shape into that of a wolf," Mulder said. He showed Scully another page in the file. It was a drawing, an artist's rendering of the Lewis and Clark report.

Scully glanced at it: a creature with a wolf's head, a human torso, and rabid eyes. The creature's fangs were tearing into a helpless white settler. The drawing was very imaginative. But not very convincing.

She closed the folder and looked at Mulder in disbelief. Did he really expect her to take this seriously?

"Mulder," she said patiently. "What this folder describes is called lycanthropy. It's a type of insanity in which an individual believes that he can turn into a wolf. Most of the old stories about werewolves were really describing people who suffered from lycanthropy. I mean, no one can physically change into an animal!"

Scully handed him the file and got out of the car. Mulder's latest theory was too ridiculous even to argue about.

She opened her umbrella and started toward the pyre. A cold wind blew down from the mountaintops. It was raining again.

Mulder caught up with her. "How can you just dismiss the evidence?" he asked. "The tracks in the mud. The shredded skin. A man with the teeth of an animal."

Scully was out of patience. "Mulder!" she shouted over the wind. "Even if you're right, even if Joe Goodensnake did somehow have the ability to actually transform into an animal, he's dead." She nodded toward the pyre. "Jim Parker shot him, and in a little while his body will be burned. End of mystery."

"Let's hope so," Mulder said.

Scully strode away from him, trying to cool off. Werewolves! Next Mulder would want to investigate vampires. Or dancing jack-o'-lanterns!

She slowed as she focused on the sight in front of her. The medicine man lighting sage incense. Joe Goodensnake's body waiting to be burned. She thought about the fangs in Goodensnake's mouth. The scars on his chest. The scars that were so similar to Lyle's wounds. The cow that had been torn apart.

Scully didn't believe for one second that Goodensnake had turned into some kind of supernatural animal. But something strange *was* going on here. And it was up to her and Mulder to find out what it was.

Chapter NINE

Dusk was falling. The sunset had turned the sky an otherworldly reddish orange. To Mulder, the flaming sky seemed to herald the fire that would soon consume Joe Goodensnake's body. At the base of the pyre, the medicine man was still praying, and the air smelled of cedar and sage. Like many Native American ceremonies, this one would go on for hours.

More people gathered to bid farewell to Joe Goodensnake. Mulder recognized the tall, gray-haired man who'd spoken to them in the pool hall. Mulder nodded to the man respectfully. But the man didn't nod back.

Scully found herself watching Gwen Goodensnake. The young woman stood alone, well away from everyone else. There were no tears in her eyes, but Scully could see her grief in the way she held her body. Gwen looked as though she were sick—and terribly, terribly alone. She stared, glassy-eyed, at the burial platform, as if she couldn't quite believe what she saw there.

Slowly Scully approached her.

Gwen didn't even turn to see who it was but said, "You don't belong here."

"Gwen—" Scully began.

"You're only here to wrap up your investigation," Gwen said in a hard, flat voice.

Scully knew this was not the time or place to argue. She started to walk away, then paused and said, "I just wanted to say that I'm sorry about your brother. I feel sad for anyone who loses a part of their family."

"A 'part'?" Gwen asked.

Scully just listened.

"He was my *whole* family," Gwen said in a broken whisper. "I'm it now."

Scully stood silently beside the grieving woman. She felt helpless. She wished she could do something to comfort Gwen. But as a stranger and an outsider, there wasn't a lot she could say. Especially since she knew Gwen was right. If it hadn't been for the case, she and Mulder wouldn't have been there.

Gwen turned to face her. She seemed to be gathering courage for her next words. "As a demonstration of sorrow, I'm supposed to give away all of my brother's possessions," she said.

She held out a handmade beaded bracelet. It was decorated with feathers, two bear claws, and a mountain lion's tooth. Scully didn't know much about Native American traditions, but she did know that both bear claws and teeth from a mountain lion were considered symbols of courage. Joe Goodensnake must have been a very brave man.

Scully was surprised and moved when Gwen handed her the bracelet. "Gwen . . . I . . . I don't know what to say," she protested.

"It's no big deal." Gwen's voice was suddenly bitter. "My brother had more possessions than friends." Then, before Scully could say anything else, Gwen walked away from her, blinking back tears.

Mulder was the first to notice Charlie Tskany driving up in his Jeep. Tskany got out, looking slightly ill at ease. Beneath his sheriff's parka, he wore a dark suit and a bolo tie. He stood back from the mourners, watching the pyre.

Mulder went to stand beside him. "I read the report of your investigation into the Goodensnake homicide," he said. "It was very good. Thorough. Professional. But what I want to know is off the record. . . . What do you really think happened?"

The sheriff gave Mulder a sideways glance. "Your explanation, Agent Mulder, is lying on that burial platform," he replied. "Why don't you just accept that and go home?"

Still Mulder couldn't give up. He knew the investigation might be over. Which meant this might be his only chance to ask. "Charlie . . . do you believe in shape-shifting?"

Tskany refused to meet Mulder's gaze. He kept his eyes on the pyre. "This is a funeral," he said.

When the last rays of the sun were gone, a torch was lit. The medicine man lowered the torch to the wood. Orange flames leaped toward the crystal stars above. Smoke curled from the fire, creating a wavering, surreal haze.

As the fire crackled against the night sky, a group of men standing around a drum beat a slow, steady rhythm. Singers began to chant the songs that had been part of this ceremony for generations. To Mulder, the high-pitched songs sounded almost like cries of grief. They were eerie, ancient, beautiful.

The fire grew quickly in the wind. The sickly sweet smell of burning flesh filled the air. Over the music of the drum and the singers came the sound of hoofbeats. Mulder turned and was surprised to see Lyle Parker riding toward the funeral, dressed in a suit and tie.

Lyle stopped his horse at the edge of the clearing. He took off his hat and sat watching the ceremony from horseback.

His horse whinnied quietly. And Gwen heard it.

She turned toward the sound, and a look of rage crossed her face. She strode furiously toward Lyle. Tskany and the two FBI agents followed her at once.

"Get out of here!" she screamed.

"Please," Lyle said. "I just want to pay my respects."

"I don't want your 'respects,'" Gwen told him angrily. "I want your heart to grow cold. I want you to feel what *I'm* feeling." Too angry to go on, she spat at him.

Lyle didn't answer but lowered his eyes as if ashamed.

"I think you'd better leave, Mr. Parker," the sheriff suggested. He put a hand on Gwen's shoulder, but she brushed it off.

Lyle seemed upset. From what Scully could tell, he genuinely regretted Goodensnake's death. *Lyle meant well by coming to the funeral,* she thought. *But he'd only made things worse. And he knew it.*

He put his hat back on. "I wish your brother could be here," he said to Gwen. "I wish that more than anything else."

Gwen didn't answer. She returned to her place by the fire, not even looking up as Lyle rode off.

Mulder watched Gwen, her face lit by the flames. She was staring into the fire, grief-stricken but proud, swaying slightly to the sound of the drum.

Mulder could barely make out the shrouded body through the flames. *Was Joe Goodensnake a shape-shifter?* he wondered. *Was Parker telling the truth? Had Goodensnake turned into some kind of beast the night he was killed? Now no one would ever know. Another X-file unsolved*, Mulder thought. *Another mystery.*

He could do nothing but watch as the flames danced wildly, carrying Joe Goodensnake's spirit back to his creator.

Chapter TEN

Miles away from the funeral pyre, Jim Parker sat in the rocker on the porch of the ranch house. It was a cool, starlit night. He rocked quietly, thinking about the day. He'd mended the fence that had broken the night Lyle was attacked. He'd spent hours breaking in a new quarter horse. He'd unloaded a truckful of hay, readying the barn for winter. After a long day of ranch work, this was his favorite way to spend the evening. Sitting in his rocking chair with a mug of coffee. Watching the sun go down and the moon rise.

Darkness had fallen about an hour ago. The night sky was black and spangled with stars. He let the mug warm his hands, watching the dark liquid move to the rocking of the chair. He wondered where Lyle was. The boy had taken one of the geldings out, just after dinner. Parker hadn't seen him since.

Briefly he let his thoughts drift to Joe Goodensnake. Shooting the Indian boy had been a nasty business. Not at all what he'd intended. He could have sworn it was some kind of animal, attacking Lyle. But now his cattle were safe. And he wasn't sorry about that.

A chilly breeze whistled through his jacket. Parker pulled up his collar and listened to the sounds of the evening. Crickets chirping. Cows lowing. Horses snorting softly. Wind chimes tinkling in the breeze. The rocking chair creaking against the porch floorboards.

He sipped his coffee. Everything was peaceful tonight. Exactly the way it should be.

And then he heard it. A low, faint growl. So faint he wasn't really sure he'd heard it at all.

He stopped rocking and cocked his head to listen.

He heard only the wind chimes.

Then the breeze died down. The chimes fell silent.

Even stranger, the cows and the horses fell silent, too. And the crickets. All the sounds of the night suddenly vanished.

Parker felt a chill race up his spine. The silence was eerie. Unnatural. No night in the country was this quiet.

He wasn't going to give in to fear. He never had before, and he was too old to start now. Carefully he set down his mug.

The curved base of the rocker rolled as Parker

got to his feet. Slowly he stepped down from the porch. The leather of his cowboy boots gave a slight squeak as he walked.

Parker started toward the corral. He paused, listening to the complete stillness. Nothing. Maybe he'd imagined that growl. The things that had happened around here lately were enough to make anyone paranoid. He started back toward the house, thinking maybe it was time to get his gun.

He never heard it coming.

One second, there was silence.

The next, something was right behind him. Something powerful enough to slam him down against the stairs, facefirst.

Parker turned his head to see his attacker, despite the stabbing pain through his neck. He had faced enraged bears, she-wolves guarding their young, and even a rabid mountain lion. But he'd never seen anything like this. A two-legged creature with a hulking, hairy body. A wrinkled, leathery snout. Wild, burning red eyes. Claws like curved razors. Half beast, half man. Parker knew that this creature—whatever it was—had been murdering his cattle. And he knew that tonight it had come to murder him.

An ice-cold terror streaked through Parker's veins. The fear was even worse than the night he'd shot Joe Goodensnake. Then, he'd been trying to save his son's life. Now, he was fighting for his own.

Parker tried to run. If only he could get inside and grab his shotgun. If only he could get to a phone. If only he could put the solid wood door between himself and the creature.

Parker never had a chance.

He hadn't even taken the first step before he was thrown against the rocker with so much force that it splintered beneath him.

For a moment Parker lay stunned. Blood trickled down his forehead. The growling behind him grew into a maddened roar. Parker turned to see the beast launching itself straight at him.

Frantic, he tried to pull himself up and out of the way. His fingernails scraped against the stairs. And then he felt himself being lifted high into the air. He twisted his body around in a vain struggle to break free.

But he wasn't fast enough. Strong enough. Lucky enough.

His scream was the last sound he ever made. It echoed through the Montana night as his blood hit the ceramic mug and slid into the coffee.

Once again the unnatural silence cloaked the ranch. Until at last the breeze returned, and the wind chimes began to play a chilling song in the night air.

Chapter ELEVEN

Scully and Mulder got into their rental car the next morning and set off for the airport. Their case was now officially closed. It was time for them to get back to FBI Headquarters in Washington, D.C.

Scully was at the wheel. Mulder stared morosely out the window.

"You're glad we're going back, aren't you?" he asked.

"There isn't anything here for us," Scully said.

"And you don't think there ever was?" Mulder pressed.

Scully shrugged. "I haven't seen any real evidence that shape-shifters exist. I think this X-file dead-ended in Joe Goodensnake's funeral. But tell me something, Mulder. Let's say we had been able to prove that Goodensnake was some sort of genetic freak, capable of transforming into an animal. Then what?"

"Then maybe we could have tried to prevent it from happening again," Mulder said.

"How?" Scully asked. "That would be like trying to prevent someone from being born with blond hair. Or with hemophilia. Our understanding of genetics isn't that advanced that we can manipulate—"

"Maybe this isn't just a case of being born a freak," Mulder said. "Maybe—" He broke off as his cellular phone rang. "Mulder here," he said, into the receiver.

Scully couldn't tell what was going on from Mulder's side of the conversation. When it was over, he folded up the phone and said, "We need to make a U-turn."

"Why?" Scully asked.

"We're heading back to Two Medicine Ranch," Mulder explained. "Jim Parker's dead. They think it happened last night. From what the police can tell, he was attacked by a wild animal."

One hour later, Scully stepped out of the Parkers' ranch house. She'd just spoken with the coroner and the two Browning police officers who were on the scene.

Jim Parker's body lay on the porch, covered with a plastic tarp. Scully lifted the tarp and winced at what she saw. His death had been gruesome.

Nearby, a camera flashed as another police officer documented the crime scene. Sheriff Tskany stood at the base of the porch steps, reading through a report that one of the officers had handed him.

Scully went to talk to him. "By the way the body's been mutilated, I'd say Parker was attacked by a large predator," she said. She paused as another possibility occurred to her. "Or it was made to look that way."

Tskany remained silent.

"Sheriff, do you think this was an act of retaliation?" Scully asked. "For the death of Joe Goodensnake?"

"I don't know," Tskany said.

"Have you questioned Gwen Goodensnake?" Scully asked. "She was quite upset last night."

"She's gone," Tskany said in a flat voice. "No one has seen her since the funeral."

Scully fought down a stab of impatience. In her mind, Gwen was their prime suspect. How could the sheriff be so casual about her disappearance?

As if reading her thoughts, Tskany said, "I've put out an APB on her."

Scully nodded. Tskany might not like working with federal agents, but he was a good, thorough cop.

"And what about Lyle Parker?" Scully asked.

"We can't find him, either," Tskany admitted.

"He may be dead as well," Scully said in a worried tone. "I'll have a look around."

Tskany nodded as Scully moved away. He

started toward the covered body. He might as well have a look at the corpse.

He stopped on the first stair. His left hand, the one holding the police report, was shaking. That was when Tskany realized something he hated to admit. He didn't want to look at Parker's body. He knew exactly what he was going to find. And it terrified him.

Nearly a mile from the crime scene, Mulder was searching for evidence where no one else would look. He was up on a hill on the far edge of the corral. He moved over the area, then bent down and picked up a clump of coarse brown fur from the ground. He'd need an expert to identify it, but to him it didn't look like bear or cow or wolf or mountain lion. Mulder had never seen anything like it. And he was willing to bet that most crime labs hadn't, either.

He kept searching.

And then he spotted what he'd been looking for.

Another torn piece of translucent skin—this one in the shape of a human face.

Scully moved away from the ranch house in wider and wider circles. She didn't want to miss a clue. She was in an area near the corral where Parker kept penned animals. There were a number of wire cages holding chickens, rabbits, and a few goats.

Two golden animal eyes followed Scully as she moved. A predator's eyes, measuring her every step.

A low, throaty growl made her turn. She locked stares with a mountain lion, its tail lashing angrily.

Before she could react, the cougar sprang toward her with fangs bared—only to be stopped by the wire walls of its cage.

Scully felt her muscles ease with relief. *Why on earth would anyone cage a mountain lion?* she wondered. She thought of Parker's stuffed hunting trophies. Had he planned a similar fate for the cougar? She backed away from the growling animal, continuing her search around the ranch.

A good distance from the cougar, she saw a dark form on the ground. She was afraid of what it might be, but she ran toward it anyway.

As the shape became clearer, Scully's fear turned into regret and sadness. Lyle Parker's body lay motionless in a pool of muddy water.

Sheriff Tskany knelt and carefully lifted the plastic sheet that covered Jim Parker's body. His eyes darted over the victim. Spotting something, he reached out with his other hand and produced an object from Parker's body. He studied it, his brows drawn together in concentration.

Mulder, walking toward the porch, saw that Tskany was holding a claw. A broken, jagged, razor-sharp claw.

"That's not from any animal I've ever seen," Mulder said.

Tskany made no reply.

"Sheriff," Mulder said. "I think it's time we had a talk."

As usual, Tskany responded with silence.

"An exchange of ideas?" Mulder suggested. He tried to keep the sarcasm out of his voice, but he was getting tired of Tskany's keeping secrets while all around them people were being torn to shreds.

Tskany finally cleared his throat, as if to answer. But at that moment Scully appeared from around the side of the house. Lyle Parker was with her, wrapped in a thick horse blanket. The young man walked with difficulty. He was ghostly pale, with circles beneath his feverish eyes. And although the temperature was barely forty degrees, he was sweating.

Scully guided Lyle to the rental car and helped him into the backseat.

"I'm taking him to the hospital," she told Mulder and Tskany. "He's suffering from exposure. After he's attended to, I'll question him."

Mulder nodded as Scully got inside and tore off

down the drive. He turned back to Tskany. It was time to stop playing games. This time he was going to get answers. "What are you hiding?" he demanded.

The sheriff stared at the ground. "I thought it was over," he murmured. He seemed to be talking more to himself than to Mulder.

"Over?" Mulder echoed. "Is that why you wouldn't allow an autopsy on Joe Goodensnake? You thought it'd all end after his body was cremated? What were you afraid we'd find?"

Tskany looked at Parker's body, then finally met the FBI agent's eyes. "I can't tell you," he said. "But I'll take you to somebody who can."

Chapter TWELVE

The Grove Medical Clinic in Browning was a small two-story wooden building. In a room on the second floor, Scully waited while a nurse drew vials of blood from Lyle Parker's arm.

Scully glanced around the room. The rural hospital's decor appeared to be from the Great Depression of the 1930s. She only hoped that the clinic's technology was a good deal more modern.

When the nurse left the room, Scully approached the side of the bed. Lyle lay back against the pillows. He still looked pale and drained.

Scully wondered what had happened to him after he left Goodensnake's funeral the night before. Did he know about his father's death? Had he also been attacked by whoever—or whatever—had killed his father? And if he hadn't, then what *had* happened to him?

Lyle seemed to sense her questions. "I don't know what happened after the funeral. I was pretty shook up," he began in a soft voice. He hesitated, avoiding her eyes. "I went back to the ranch and . . . I don't remember a thing after that."

He winced, and Scully wasn't sure whether he was wincing at physical pain or his memories.

"Sometimes when I'm down," Lyle went on, "I go out to where me and my dad keep stray animals. A lot of 'em wander onto the ranch hurt or looking for food. I just watch 'em, you know. It keeps things in perspective."

Scully listened, wondering what Lyle was about to confess.

"That mountain lion out there," Lyle went on. "I could watch it pace back and forth for hours. Watch the way its muscles ripple. Look at its eyes, all golden. Those eyes don't know anything about attorneys or property disputes. . . ."

He stopped, as if he were embarrassed, but then continued. "Anyway . . . my mom, when she was alive, was the one that started keepin' those animals. I guess I go out there and think about her, too." He smiled ruefully and shook his head. "I must have been really out of it last night to run around out there like that. Must have thought I was one of those animals."

"When you came home from the funeral," Scully said, "did you talk to your father?"

Lyle thought for a moment before answering, as if he was having trouble remembering. "No. He'd have been mad that I even went to the funeral. I . . .

I have an image of him . . . sitting on the front porch . . . but I don't remember talking to him. Why?"

Scully suddenly realized that Lyle didn't know what had happened to his father. Which meant that she was the one who had to tell him.

She didn't hesitate. "Your father is dead," she said as gently as she could.

Lyle's eyes stared into hers, pleading with her to take back her words.

"I'm sorry," Scully said.

Lyle shut his eyes, and Scully could see that he was trying not to cry.

"It appears as if he's been attacked by an animal," she went on, wanting Lyle to have as much information as possible. "But I suspect it may be homicide."

Lyle took the news silently. He lay there, fists clenched, wrestling with his grief. Scully had a strict professional policy: She never got personally involved with the people in her cases. But she couldn't help feeling a deep sympathy for Lyle Parker.

"Lyle," she said gently. "I lost my father recently, and I know the overwhelming—"

"Was it my fault?" Lyle broke in, his eyes still shut.

The question caught Scully off guard.

"By going to the funeral," Lyle said. "Did I anger them into killing my father?"

"I don't know," Scully answered truthfully.

Lyle looked as though something inside him had been broken. "I can deal with death, you know," he said. "Livin' on the ranch, close to nature and all, you see how it all works. Things are born. Things die. Everything else falls in between. I can accept that."

Scully nodded.

"But if I caused it, if I brought it on . . . I . . ." He was fighting tears as he spoke. "I couldn't . . . I—"

He broke down then and began to cry in long, anguished sobs. Scully put a comforting hand on his arm. There was a lot she could say, but nothing she could do. Except allow Lyle Parker time to grieve.

Chapter THIRTEEN

Mulder figured he and Charlie Tskany had been driving for about an hour since leaving Two Medicine Ranch. Tskany hadn't said a single word. Not about Jim Parker's death. Or about where they were going. Or about whoever it was they were going to meet.

About ten minutes earlier, Tskany had pulled off a two-lane highway onto a dirt road that ran through the woods. Now he turned off the dirt road and pulled up in front of a narrow log cabin.

A bleached cow skull hung from one of the posts that supported the roof. Beneath the skull, colored strips of cloth called prayer ties fluttered in the wind. Mulder recognized the colors of the sacred six directions: yellow for the east, white for the south, black for the west, red for the north, blue for the sky above, and green for the earth below. Mulder had once watched a Lakota medicine man fasten prayer ties to the inside of a sweat lodge. Each time he'd tied one, he'd said a prayer to the spirits of that direction.

A cord of firewood was stacked at the side of the

house. Automobile shells and rusted motorcycles dotted the property. The only working vehicle seemed to be an old pickup.

Tskany parked beside the pickup, and he and Mulder got out. "This is Ish's place," Tskany said.

Before Mulder could ask who Ish was, the door opened.

The gray-haired man from the pool hall stood gazing at them with calm, clear eyes. He was not at all surprised to see them. In fact, Mulder would have bet money that he'd been expecting their visit.

Ish motioned for Tskany and Mulder to follow him inside. They entered one long room, divided into a kitchen and a bedroom area. The house was lit by candles and a few small lamps. Mulder smelled the sweet, clean scent of cedar incense.

It was the house of a thoughtful man, Mulder saw. Stacks of books were everywhere. A twin bed was covered with a wool blanket, woven in a geometric Navajo pattern. A ceremonial medicine shield, the sort that used to be carried into battle as a protection, hung from one wall.

A large poster of Sitting Bull hung from another. Sitting Bull was a Sioux leader who'd taken part in an 1868 peace treaty with the U.S. government. When the government later violated the terms of that treaty, Sitting Bull led the Indian warriors in

65

the attack that defeated General Custer's army at the Battle of Little Bighorn.

For Mulder the poster was another reminder of the long, bitter history of relations between Native Americans and the U.S. government. He knew that the government had betrayed the Indians again and again. He didn't blame Ish for not trusting a government agent. He only hoped that Ish might help them anyway—since the killer on the loose was attacking white men and Tregos alike.

Ish offered Mulder and Tskany mugs of steaming herb tea. Then he sat down on the faded rug that covered the floorboards. He gestured for the two law officers to do the same.

He didn't bother to ask why they'd come. He already knew.

"I saw it once," he began. "With my own eyes. It was a long time ago. So long, it seems like a dream. I was a boy."

Mulder began to run through the X-file in his head. "In 1946?" he asked. "The Watkins case?"

Ish nodded, looking impressed. "I sensed you were different, FBI. You're more open to Native American belief than some Native Americans."

Tskany looked away. The remark was clearly meant for him.

The old man turned back to Mulder. "You even

have an Indian name . . . Fox. You should be Running Fox or Sneaky Fox."

A ghost of a smile flitted across Mulder's face. "Just as long as it's not Spooky Fox," he said.

"You know about the six sacred directions?" Ish asked him.

Mulder nodded, wondering why Ish had changed the subject. But he answered, naming the directions in the order that they were addressed in a sweat lodge. "East, south, west, north, the sky above, and earth below."

"Yes," Ish said. "And there's a seventh. That's the one you need to follow, FBI."

Mulder looked at him curiously.

"The seventh direction is the one that's sometimes hardest to find." Ish put his hand over his chest. "It's *inside*. The heart. That's the direction you must follow."

Mulder was silent for a moment. He'd spent his entire life trying to follow the seventh direction. He'd trusted his own instincts, even when everyone else thought he was crazy. It had earned him ridicule. But it had also brought him to the X-files. To this place.

"Tell me, Ish," Mulder said. "What did you see?"

Ish sighed, digging back in his memory. "Watkins had once been attacked by an animal when he was alone in the woods," he explained. "His scars healed. It was forgotten. Then the murders began.

"The Tregos, we realized that Watkins had been attacked by what the Algonquians call a manitou. *Manitou* is a word that means the mysterious power that is everywhere in nature. But it can also be the word for an evil spirit capable of changing a man into a beast. To be attacked by a manitou causes the victim to become a manitou."

"The healed scars on Joe Goodensnake's body . . . ," Mulder said.

Ish nodded. "Like the scars on Watkins's body. They were both attacked by a manitou and both became one. The manitou overtakes a man by night," he explained. "Not by full moon, but when its blood lust builds to an uncontrollable level. Then the man changes to a sickening creature. It kills, releasing the savage energy. The man later returns to his true self, unaware of what has happened. The cycle begins anew the next day. This continues until death."

Mulder glanced at Tskany, wondering if the sheriff believed what the older man was telling them.

Ish stared straight ahead as he spoke, as if he were gazing into the past. "One night when I was sixteen years old," he continued, "I was coming back from fishing in the Cut Bank Creek. I knew a short-cut behind Watkins's house. I heard a groan . . . not animal, but not human. I looked into his window. He was covered in sweat and blood. He was in great, great pain. His arm . . . the skin ripped open. It tore off and fell to the floor. . . ."

Mulder thought about the pieces of skin he'd found on the ranch.

"Claws sprang from his fingernails," Ish went on. "He turned, screaming. And he saw me! His eyes . . ."

The old man shut his own eyes, as if he couldn't bear to remember what he'd seen that day. He was silent for a long while, and Mulder feared he wouldn't finish the story.

At last Ish opened his eyes. When he spoke, his voice was calm, as though he'd fought some inner battle and won. "Watkins . . . his eyes were still human. They begged me to kill him. And if I'd been hunting and had my gun, I'd have done it without a second thought. But being a boy and scared to death . . . I ran away."

"And shortly after, the police killed him," Mulder guessed.

Ish nodded. "But the manitou rose again."

"Eight years later," Mulder said. "But with Watkins dead, how could there have been an attack by a manitou?"

"Watkins had a son," Ish answered. "It can be passed along bloodlines, too."

Mulder looked at Tskany, and for the first time since entering Ish's house, Tskany spoke.

"Gwen," he said.

It was a possibility Mulder didn't like at all.

"If Joe Goodensnake was this creature," Tskany said, "then perhaps it didn't originate in him by an earlier attack but was handed down through bloodlines. This means Gwen could have it also. Gwen could have killed Jim Parker."

Chapter FOURTEEN

The grating sound of a sputtering car engine cut through the quiet of Ish's house. Tskany was the first to pull his gun. Mulder sprang to his feet, his own gun drawn. Ish reached around and from somewhere beneath the bed produced a rifle that had to be a hundred years old.

Quietly the three men let themselves out through the back door. Tskany headed for the area near the barn. Mulder motioned for Ish to stay back and started for the front of the house.

Mulder felt his heart pounding. Maybe it was from listening to Ish's stories about spirits who could turn a man into a beast. Maybe it was from seeing Jim Parker's mangled body. But he couldn't shake the sense that they were dealing with an evil that couldn't be destroyed. And it was very close by.

He gazed around the maze of old cars and car parts in Ish's yard. There were dozens of places to hide.

He tensed as he heard a faint metallic *plink*, followed by the unmistakable sound of a car's engine.

Mulder whirled around. Someone was crouched

down behind the steering wheel of Ish's truck. And he or she was trying to hot-wire the ignition.

Mulder started toward the vehicle, his weapon drawn. A gray plume of exhaust filled the air as the truck's engine finally turned over. The driver sat up.

"Gwen!" shouted Tskany, as he and Mulder raced for the truck.

Gwen's dark eyes widened with fear as she saw the two law officers. There were too many other vehicles in Ish's yard for her to get out easily. Panicked, she threw the truck into reverse. The wheels of the truck squealed as she backed it up in a tight angle.

Tskany reached her first. He jumped onto the truck's running board, reached through the open window, and pulled the gearshift into park.

"No!" Gwen screamed, her voice filled with ter- ror. She was hysterical, Mulder saw, kicking, screaming, fighting as Tskany yanked open the door and pulled her out onto the muddy ground.

Mulder trained his gun on her, sure she would bolt.

"Gwen, you're under arrest for trying to steal Ish's truck," Tskany said sternly.

Gwen looked like a wild woman. She was wear- ing the same clothes she'd worn the night before to her brother's funeral. Her jeans were mud-stained.

Her long, brown hair was tousled and tangled with twigs and dried leaves. Her skin was streaked with tears and sweat.

Ish approached the trembling woman. "What happened, Gwen?" he asked. "What are you running away from?"

Gwen was on her knees, weeping. "I saw it!" she sobbed. "I saw it kill Parker."

Tskany looked at Mulder, his shotgun aimed at the young woman.

Slowly Mulder lowered his own gun. "Let her up," he said.

Tskany lifted Gwen to her feet. She stood slowly, then clung to him, terrified. For a long while she just sobbed into the sheriff's jacket, crying too hard to talk.

"I went to the ranch," she finally admitted. "After the funeral. I was gonna mess up the kid. And so I waited, but Parker was on the porch. And then this thing, this animal . . ." She covered her face as she sobbed. "I've never been so scared. I ran and I hid in the woods all day. I just wanted to get out. I wanted to get out of here. . . ." She broke down then, weeping so hard she couldn't go on.

Tskany looked to Mulder, but it was Ish who took control. "Bring her inside," he said.

Mulder followed them, puzzling over this latest

development. *Was Gwen telling the truth?* he wondered. Ish had said that after the manitou kills, the person has no memory of ever having been such a monster or of killing others. But Gwen said she'd seen it kill. And it had left her terrified, almost shattered.

All of which led Mulder to believe that she was telling the truth. And if she was, a frightening question remained: If Gwen wasn't the manitou, then who was?

Chapter FIFTEEN

Ish led Gwen inside the cabin. He wrapped a blanket around her shoulders. "Sit down," he told the frightened young woman. "I'll make you a cup of tea."

Charlie Tskany knelt by her side. "I need to ask you some questions," he said. "About Joe and how he got those scars on his chest."

Gwen nodded. She seemed a little calmer now. "It was a while ago," she said. "Joe went up to the top of Black Mountain for *hanbleceya*."

Mulder recognized the Lakota word for "vision quest." Vision quest was an ancient tradition. Joe Goodensnake would have spent four days and nights on the mountain, with no bedding, no food, and little water. He would have tried to stay awake the entire time, praying for a spiritual vision.

"When he came down from the mountain," Gwen said, "he had three deep, bloody gouge marks in his shoulder. I asked him what had happened. He just laughed and said he'd tangled with a spirit."

"It was the truth," Ish said.

Mulder wasted no time. He immediately grabbed

the phone and called the hospital where Scully had taken Lyle Parker. He wanted her to know what Gwen had seen at the ranch the night before. What Ish had told him about the Watkins case. And what had happened to Joe Goodensnake.

"I'm trying to reach Federal Agent Dana Scully," Mulder told the hospital receptionist. "She brought in a young man named Lyle Parker this morning."

After being put on hold for what seemed like an hour, Mulder finally heard the sound of a phone ringing and someone picking up.

"Scully?" he said.

"This is Dr. Josephs," said a male voice on the other end of the line.

"Yeah, this is Agent Mulder from the FBI," Mulder explained quickly. "I was told I could reach Agent Scully at this number."

"Oh, yes," the doctor said. "We released Lyle Parker from the hospital. She's taking him back to the ranch."

"So I can reach her there?" Mulder asked.

"They just left," Dr. Josephs said. "Agent Mulder, there's something I feel you should know. I just received the blood tests performed on Lyle Parker, and there is something rather unsettling."

"What's that?" Mulder asked. He had a terrible feeling that he already knew the answer.

"Traces of his father's blood type," the doctor answered. "It could only be there through ingestion."

Mulder stood absolutely still as the meaning of the doctor's words sank in. *Through ingestion—through eating.* Gwen was telling the truth. She wasn't the shape-shifter.

Lyle Parker was.

He'd been attacked by a manitou and had become one.

Lyle Parker was the one who had killed his father.

Mulder realized he was still holding the phone to his ear. "Thank you for your help," he said to the doctor, and hung up.

Mulder glanced out through the window. In the western sky, a blazing red sun began to set. It filled the cabin with an eerie red glow.

Mulder knew that it would be dark within the hour. In his mind, he heard Ish's words: "The manitou overtakes a man by night. . . . The man changes to a sickening creature. . . . It kills. . . . The man returns to his true self, unaware of what has happened. The cycle begins anew the next day."

Lyle Parker had killed last night. This morning he'd had no idea of what had happened. Tonight he would kill again. And now he was alone with Scully.

☠   ☠   ☠

Scully drove along a straight stretch of road, heading west. In the passenger seat Lyle slumped against the window, asleep. Scully knew that his body was still hurting from whatever had attacked him the night before. And his heart was still aching over the death of his father. She wondered what would happen to him now. Would he keep the ranch? Try to run it on his own? Or would it be too painful for him to remain there with the memories of his father?

Beside her Lyle stirred. Slowly his eyes opened. He stared out the window. If he had turned to Scully, she would have noticed the difference. Lyle Parker's eyes were changing. Something new was coming into them. Something terrifyingly inhuman.

But Scully had no idea. She kept driving toward the ranch. In the distance a bloodred sun began to set.

Chapter SIXTEEN

The sun was sinking behind the mountains. The last sliver of orange light vanished from the sky just as Scully and Lyle Parker reached Two Medicine Ranch.

Scully was tired after the long drive back from the hospital. Still, she wanted to make sure that Lyle was safely settled in the house before she left to check in with Mulder.

Beside her Lyle was silent. She hoped he was still sleeping. He needed all the rest he could get.

She stopped the car at the ranch gate, got out, unlatched it, drove through, and carefully closed the gate behind them again. *The blue light of dusk makes the ranch look almost ghostly,* Scully thought, as she drove down the long, dusty road that led to the house. In the east a full moon was rising.

Scully parked in front of the house. She shook Lyle's shoulder. "Lyle, wake up," she said. "You're home now."

"Uh-huh," Lyle said, sounding groggy. Slowly he got out of the car. He looked around him, shaking his head, as if he couldn't believe what had happened here. Moving like an old man, he let them into the house. Inside, the final bluish haze of twilight filled the spacious rooms. The house felt cold and empty.

A shaft of moonlight streamed through the door and lit a bear's head mounted high on the wall. Its open mouth cast eerie shadows on the floor. Scully had no problem with people who hunted to eat. But it bothered her to see all these animals that had been hunted as trophies. She shivered. It wasn't scary. And it didn't give her the creeps. But it did make her uncomfortable. You only had to look at any wall of the ranch house and you saw evidence of people's killing for pleasure.

Lyle closed the door behind them. He flicked on the light switch.

Nothing happened. The room was still shadowy and dim.

"Power's out," Scully said.

"Yeah." Lyle sounded weary. "It happens to us all the time, bein' out here in the sticks." He reached for a flashlight. "I'll fire up the generator."

But he hadn't gone three steps before his knees buckled. He doubled over beside the stairway, gasping with pain.

Scully rushed to his side. "You okay?" she asked.

Lyle's forehead was beaded with sweat. He was

panting as though he'd just run a race. Scully watched, concerned, as he struggled to stand.

"I feel sick," Lyle said. "Please. Help me to the bathroom. . . ."

A lone Jeep tore across the night, red and blue police lights flashing from its roof. Inside, Charlie Tskany drove as Mulder punched a number into his cellular phone.

Mulder listened patiently, waiting for the phone at Two Medicine Ranch to ring. He heard one ring followed by the loud crackle of static.

Mulder grimaced and hit End. Then he tried the number again. And got more static.

Frustrated, Mulder shut off the phone. "It keeps disconnecting," he told the sheriff. "The mountains must be blocking the signal. How much farther?"

" 'Bout seven miles," Tskany answered. He hit the gas pedal, taking the Jeep well over the speed limit.

The only light in the ranch house was Scully's flashlight. She stood in the hallway outside the bathroom door. Inside, she heard Lyle retching violently.

"Lyle," she called. "Let me come in."

The was no response, only the sound of Lyle's labored breathing.

Scully knew that Lyle hadn't been this sick when they'd left the hospital. What had happened since then? Was he just in shock at being back at the ranch after his father's death? Or was there something wrong that the doctors had missed?

She heard Lyle throwing up again.

She called to him to let her in.

And again there was no answer.

Scully tried the door. It was locked.

Lyle stood inside the tiny bathroom. He leaned against the sink, holding himself upright. Though the house was cold, his body was slick with sweat. He was burning up with fever. Every second, it got harder to breathe.

He tore off his jacket. But it didn't help. Sweat was pouring down his back and chest. His throat was so dry, he could barely swallow. And now he was in pain. More pain than he'd ever been in before. It felt as though something inside him were tearing apart.

He heard Agent Scully rattling the door again.

"Lyle?" she called.

He raised his head. Daring a glance in the mirror, he opened his eyes. Moonlight streamed in through the bathroom window. Enough light to see that his eyes—the irises *and* the pupils—were bloodred.

☠   ☠   ☠

Scully stood in the hallway, waiting for Lyle to answer her. She was really worried about him now.

She tried one more time. "Lyle, answer me!"

She was done waiting.

She knelt and examined the doorknob. Two screws held it in place. Scully reached into her pocket and took out the small utility knife she always carried. Quickly she began to unscrew the metal plate around the doorknob.

Inside the bathroom, Lyle was doubled over with pain. It got worse by the second. Hot, stabbing waves of pain. Something was ripping at his insides.

He looked up to see the brass plate around the doorknob beginning to move.

He heard Agent Scully on the other side of the door. "Lyle, listen to me," she said. "I want to take you back to the hospital, okay?"

"No, I'll be all right," he called back. He wiped his mouth with his sleeve. He turned on the cold water. He'd feel better in a moment. He had to. It couldn't get worse.

Cupping his hands, he brought the water to his parched mouth. Again and again.

He paused, hand over his mouth. He felt so sick.

He leaned over the toilet and tried to throw up. His stomach heaved, but nothing came up.

He was so hot, he felt as if he were standing in front of a furnace. He tore off his shirt. The claw marks on his shoulder were covered with bandages, but he could feel them, each one stinging like a red-hot knife. What was happening to him?

Whatever it was, it was out of his control. He doubled over, then arched his spine backward. For a second the pain eased, and Lyle straightened up. Or tried to. Instead his head whipped back and his mouth opened wide in agony.

Only it wasn't a scream that came out—it was a low, rumbling growl.

"Lyle!" The woman's voice was still calling. "What's going on in there? Are you all right? Please, just open the door!"

For the last time, Lyle thought about what he'd say to her. How to explain what was happening inside him. And then his thoughts vanished and something else took over.

He risked another glance in the mirror. A howl rose from his throat—and in the mirror's reflection he saw four pointed fangs in his open mouth.

He heard sounds on the other side of the door. And smelled another creature. He reached for the window and raked his hand down the curtain.

Razor-sharp claws sliced through the cotton fabric.

Lyle heard himself roaring. Like a wounded mountain lion. Like an animal gone mad with pain.

He clenched his fist and looked on in horror. The flesh on the back of his hand split open.

And a three-fingered piece of translucent skin dropped to the floor.

Chapter SEVENTEEN

Charlie Tskany's Jeep barreled down the road to the ranch. They were almost there. And yet for Mulder, they weren't close enough. Night had fallen. Thick clouds hid the full moon. The Montana landscape was blanketed in darkness.

Which meant the spirit of the manitou would be taking over, Mulder realized. Lyle Parker wouldn't be Lyle Parker anymore. He'd be a deadly beast whose only impulse was to destroy.

Tskany pulled up in front of the gate that led into the ranch. Mulder bolted out of the Jeep, opened the gate, and jumped back in.

Tskany drove through the open gate and stopped.

"What are you stopping for?" Mulder demanded.

"You've got to close the gate," Tskany told him.

"Forget about the gate," Mulder snapped. "Scully's in there alone with Lyle."

Tskany gave him a look of disgust, got out, quickly shut the gate behind them, and got back into the truck.

"Do you want to tell me what that was all about?" Mulder asked angrily.

"You leave the gate open, the cattle are going to wander out and onto the road," Tskany told him. "It only takes a few seconds to shut the gate. And it saves livestock. You grow up in this part of the country, you close gates."

Mulder was tempted to point out that saving livestock might well cost Scully her life. But Tskany was accelerating through the gears like a race-car driver. The Jeep sped down the dirt road and screeched to a stop in front of the house.

Mulder's heart sank as he looked at the ranch house. The rental car was parked in front of the steps. Scully and Lyle were definitely here.

And something was definitely wrong.

The ranch house was completely dark.

In the hallway, Scully worked frantically to remove the last screw from the doorknob. The sounds coming from the bathroom were awful. What was happening to Lyle? It almost sounded as if the mountain lion had broken out of its cage and had somehow gotten in there with him.

The screw loosened, then fell to the floor. She pulled out the knob and was about to open the lock.

But she never got a chance. A deafening roar filled the house, and the bathroom door splintered apart.

Scully found herself flying backward. She never even saw the enraged creature that burst out into the hall. Her head hit the wall behind her. And then everything went black.

Within seconds Mulder and Tskany were out of the Jeep. The sheriff was holding his shotgun, Mulder his automatic.

The ranch was silent. Mulder saw no signs of violence. But he and Tskany exchanged worried glances. It was too quiet. They should have been able to hear the ranch animals. Coyotes. Owls. Insects. It felt as if everything on the land were hiding. Or dead.

Mulder signaled for Tskany to check the back of the house. Then he hurried toward the front door.

The door opened easily. It was unlocked. Carefully, quietly, Mulder entered the ranch house. Inside, it was pitch black.

Mulder flicked on the light switch. Nothing. The power was out.

He waited a moment for his eyes to adjust to the darkness. He didn't want to use his flashlight unless it was necessary. If the creature was nearby, the flashlight beam would advertise Mulder as convenient food.

A thin shaft of moonlight filtered in through the

blinds of one of the windows. There was no sign of Scully or Lyle. Or of any disturbance. Everything seemed to be in its place. The room was peaceful. And yet, like the silence outside, the peace inside the house was unsettling.

Mulder was both puzzled and wary. The rental car was in front of the house, he reminded himself. That meant Scully and Lyle had to be here somewhere.

He went past the foot of the stairway, deciding to explore the downstairs first. He crept down the hallway, touching the wall with one hand and holding his gun in the other.

Mulder froze as his fingertips felt a break in the texture of the wooden paneling. For just a second, he shone his flashlight on the wall. It was long enough to see that the wood was gouged with three deep scratches.

Mulder looked about, readied his gun, and started across the room. He bumped into something, hitting his shin hard. He flashed on the light to see what he'd bumped into.

It was a footstool—with a piece of translucent skin hanging over the edge.

Mulder's heart was pounding. He moved toward the bathroom. And what he saw there frightened him even more than the shred of skin: a beam of light. Scully's flashlight lay on the floor, shining down the other end of the hallway.

But there was no sign of Scully.

A vision of Jim Parker's mangled corpse flashed through Mulder's mind. He edged toward the flashlight and picked it up.

When he spoke, his voice was a hoarse whisper. "Scully . . ."

Chapter EIGHTEEN

Mulder searched the darkened hallway for a clue to his partner's whereabouts. A piece of Scully's clothing. A strand of her hair. Anything that would tell him where she was. Or what had happened to her.

A low, rumbling growl stopped Mulder cold. He spun toward the sound. He knew enough about animals to know that the deeper the growl, the larger the animal. The sound he'd just heard was a good deal deeper than the mountain lion's. Whatever had made it was much bigger and much more dangerous.

Mulder inched back down the hallway. His flashlight skimmed along the frame of the kitchen door. Nothing.

He heard the growling again. Louder this time. As if it rose from the earth itself. Mulder could feel the sound vibrating along his spine.

The manitou was close. Very close.

Mulder had no choice. He had to find Scully.

He continued his search.

☠   ☠   ☠

Outside, Charlie Tskany shone his flashlight beam around the back of the house. Nothing unusual. Except the quiet.

Tskany had grown up in this part of the country. He'd lived here all his life. He'd worked on a ranch and in a national park before he became a law officer. He'd spent more nights outdoors than he could count. And yet he'd never heard a night so silent.

It wasn't natural.

It terrified him.

He thought of Ish's tale of the manitou. It was the sort of story Tskany had believed as a boy, and laughed at as a man. But Ish never lied. And Tskany had seen the proof. Whatever he was hunting was neither animal nor man, but something evil and far more deadly.

Tskany edged toward the corral. He froze as he heard a sound. He listened for it again and heard something that might be an animal—and might not.

A low, fierce growling sound.

Instantly he flicked on his flashlight.

In the center of the strong, white beam, a caged mountain lion bared its fangs and hissed.

Tskany was almost relieved.

The manitou was close. He could feel it. Somewhere in the darkness, it was waiting for him.

☠   ☠   ☠

Mulder stepped into the kitchen. He heard another mysterious growl, but it was impossible to tell where it came from. Or who was hunting whom.

He let his light scan the kitchen: counters, cabinets, sink, refrigerator, wooden trestle table and chairs. Nothing out of the ordinary.

And then he heard it again. The low animal rumble. He shone the light in the direction of the sound. He whirled just in time to glimpse something darting across the living room and disappearing through the doorway. It was two-legged. Huge. Covered with a thick pelt.

Mulder went after the creature at once, his weapon raised. *What happened to Scully?* he wondered as he followed it toward the stairway.

He climbed the stairs, hurried but cautious. The floorboards creaked with every step. As he neared the top of the flight he felt something behind him.

Years of training as an FBI agent took over. In one smooth move Mulder spun low and fired.

There was no answering sound. No cry of pain. No body falling to the floor.

Mulder turned on the flashlight again and saw exactly what he'd fired on: fangs. Long, yellow, and poised to kill. It was the mounted head of the grizzly bear, frozen in the moment of attack. And he'd just blown off part of its jaw.

Terrific, Mulder thought. *The FBI achieves a stunning victory over a stuffed animal.*

His breath caught as he heard it again. The low growl. Like thunder before the storm. And it was upstairs. Definitely upstairs.

Mulder continued up the stairs, reaching the second floor. He was getting closer to it. He could feel it. He wondered where Tskany was. And where on earth was Scully? Was she still alive?

The second-floor hallway stretched both right and left. It was pitch black in both directions. Mulder paused for a moment, his heart hammering. Which way should he go? Where was the manitou?

Mulder started to the right. He'd gone only a few feet when something suddenly shot out from the darkness and clamped around his arm.

Mulder knew instantly that it was a human hand that had closed like iron around his wrist. Still, he was caught off balance as it yanked him into a dark room.

He struggled to pull away and aim his gun in the darkness.

"Mulder, it's me," Scully whispered. "It's me! Don't fire."

Mulder felt a flash of anger at having been frightened so badly. But mostly he was glad to see his partner alive.

And he was worried about her. "Are you okay?" he asked.

"I don't know what happened," Scully answered. "Something jumped me downstairs. I think I was knocked out for a few minutes. I lost my gun."

"I heard the creature come up here," he told her.

He started out of the room. Scully followed him.

They began to search the second floor. Methodically the two agents went from room to room, all of them bathed in shadows. They entered one that looked like Lyle's bedroom. Another that had been his father's. They checked the closets. A wardrobe. The second-floor bath.

Suddenly the sound of rasping breath drew Mulder's attention to a door at the end of the hall-way.

He and Scully approached the door. It was ajar. They stopped, listening to a labored, rhythmic breathing.

Slowly Mulder pushed open the door. The hinges creaked.

Like the rest of the house, the room was dark. Mulder gestured for Scully to follow as he stepped inside. He switched on his light and saw that they were in an office. The flashlight beam revealed a desk and chair on the wall closest to the door. Across from them was a window and a door covered with blinds. Mulder guessed the door led to an outside deck. Bookshelves, plaques on the wall, and more of the mounted game animals decorated the room.

The two agents separated, each of them trying to see into the dark. Each of them searching for the creature who'd killed Jim Parker.

But neither of them seeing the monstrous form crouching in the shadows.

Or its glowing red eyes.

Chapter NINETEEN

The creature moved like lightning. One second, the room was deathly still. The next, a furious roar erupted behind the two agents.

Mulder and Scully spun around to confront it. Mulder felt an odd disbelief as a huge, fur-covered creature with glowing red eyes and razor claws launched itself at them.

Mulder raised his gun with both hands and aimed.

A flash of light cut through the darkness.

And the sound of a gunshot echoed through the room.

A man's anguished cry rose up as the force of the gunshot drove the creature against the wall. There was a dull thud as its body hit the floor. Then it slumped in the shadows, dead.

Mulder turned to the doorway, amazed. He hadn't fired the shot that killed the manitou. Someone else had.

Charlie Tskany stood in the doorway, emptying the shells from his shotgun. He looked up at Mulder and Scully. "You all right?" he asked, stepping into the room.

Mulder nodded. "Thanks," he said.

He and Tskany shone their lights on the dark heap that had been the manitou.

But there was no sign of the fierce creature who'd attacked Mulder.

Instead they saw Lyle Parker.

The young man lay dead from a shotgun wound in his chest.

It was exactly what Mulder and Tskany had expected. But not Scully.

"Oh my God!" she gasped. She moved to the boy's body. "He was in the bathroom, sick," she said. "Then, next thing I knew, we were attacked by the mountain lion . . . out back . . . It must have gotten loose. . . ."

Mulder and Tskany exchanged glances, as if to ask each other, "How do you explain it?"

Mulder came to stand beside his partner. "It wasn't the mountain lion, Scully," he said gently.

At first she didn't understand.

"The lion's still in the cage out back," Tskany added.

Scully nodded, but she looked dazed. As if she didn't—or couldn't—believe the horrific reality in front of her.

Early the next morning Mulder and Scully left the Trego Tribal Police Office. They had just finished filing written reports on the case. Mulder glanced up as he walked down the stairs. The skies were gray. It was threatening to rain again. But things felt very different from the first time they'd visited the station. Then, he hadn't been sure whether Charlie Tskany would work with them or against them. Last night Tskany had saved their lives.

Now the sheriff joined them as they walked toward their rental car. Mulder looked around.

"Where's Gwen?" he asked. "She said she'd come see us before we left."

"She took off last night," Tskany answered. "Gave away all her possessions to her friends."

"She just pulled up stakes and left?" Mulder said. "Why would she do that?"

Tskany shrugged. "Her brother's gone. No family. The trouble with Parker is all over. . . ." His dark eyes looked at Scully. "Maybe she saw something she wasn't ready to understand."

"Maybe," Scully said.

Mulder studied his partner curiously. Scully had seen proof of shape-shifting with her own eyes. He wondered if she'd ever admit to it.

The two agents shook hands with Tskany and walked to their car.

As Mulder opened the car door, he heard a familiar voice call out, "FBI."

Ish, in a fringed leather jacket, was standing on a porch across from the sheriff's office. "See you in about eight years," he called out.

"I hope not," Mulder replied.

Smiling, Ish watched them go.

Mulder got into the car and started the engine. Then he and Scully began the long drive off the reservation, leaving the mountains, the mists, and their mysteries far behind.

TOP SECRET

CLASSIFIED

FOR INFORMATION ABOUT THE OFFICIAL X-FILES FAN CLUB CONTACT:

Creation Entertainment
411 N. Central Avenue
Suite 300
Glendale, CA 91203
(818) 409-0960

(This notice is inserted as a service to readers. HarperCollins Publishers is
in no way connected with this organization professionally or commercially.)

For more information about The X-Files or HarperCollins books
visit our web site at: http://www.harpercollins.com/kids

THE X FILES ™